READ BY YOURSELF

BIG BEAR
AND THE MISSING MOUSE

Written by Dugald Steer

Illustrated by John Blackman

| •PARRAGON• |

Today is a very hot day. Big Bear and Morris Mouse are going for a swim in the river.

Morris Mouse is very **quiet**.
He dives into the river. **Plop**!

Big Bear is very **noisy**.
He dives into the river. **Splash**!

Big Bear likes the water.
He likes to make
big waves.

Look out, Morris Mouse! **Whoosh!**

Big Bear is tired of swimming now. He has gone to sleep under a tree. He's a **noisy** sleeper, too!

When Big Bear wakes up,
it is the afternoon. It is
time to go home,
but Big Bear
cannot find his
little friend.

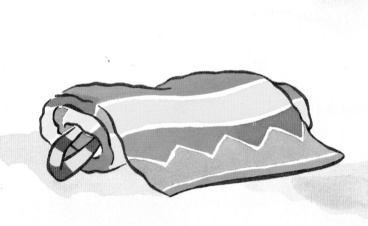

Where are you
Morris Mouse?

Big Bear is looking for his
friend. He hears a noise.
Tap! Tap! Tap!
Is that you Morris Mouse?

No, it's me Boris Badger.
I'm mending my fence.
Tap! Tap! Tap!

Where are you Morris Mouse?

They are looking for their friend. They hear a noise. **Munch! Munch! Munch!**

Is that you
Morris Mouse?

No. It's me, Percy Pig. I'm having my tea. **Munch! Munch! Munch!**

Where are
you Morris Mouse?

They are looking for their friend. They hear a noise. **La! La! La!** Is that you Morris Mouse?

No. it's me, Olive Owl.
I'm practising my singing.
La! La! Laaa!

What's this? Why, it is Morris Mouse, quite safe and sound.

But...**shhh!** Be very **quiet!**

A PARRAGON BOOK

Published by Parragon Books,
Unit 13-17, Avonbridge Trading Estate,
Atlantic Road, Avonmouth, Bristol BS 11 9QD.

Produced by The Templar Company plc,
Pippbrook Mill, London Road, Dorking, Surrey RH4 1JE.

Designed by Janie Louise Hunt

Printed and bound in Italy

ISBN 1-75250-978-0